ALFIE

Alfie's Christmas

For Brenda, with love

Other titles in the Alfie series:

Alfie Gets in First
Alfie's Feet
Alfie Gives a Hand
An Evening at Alfie's
Alfie and the Birthday Surprise
Alfie Wins a Prize
Alfie and the Big Boys
All About Alfie

Alfie's Weather
Alfie's Numbers
Alfie's Alphabet
Alfie's World
Annie Rose Is My Little Sister
Rhymes for Annie Rose
The Big Alfie and Annie Rose Storybook
The Big Alfie Out of Doors Storybook

RED FOX

UK | USA | Canada | Ireland | Australia | India | New Zealand | South Africa
Red Fox is part of the Penguin Random House group of companies
whose addresses can be found at global.penguinrandomhouse.com.
www.penguin.co.uk   www.puffin.co.uk   www.ladybird.co.uk

The Bodley Head edition published 2013, 2016
Red Fox edition published 2014
001
Copyright © Shirley Hughes, 2013
The moral right of the author has been asserted
Set in Horley Old Style MT regular
Printed in China
A CIP catalogue record for this book is available from the British Library
ISBN: 978–1–782–30064–9
All correspondence to: Red Fox, Penguin Random House Children's, 80 Strand, London WC2R 0RL

MIX
Paper from
responsible sources
FSC® C018179

Penguin Random House is committed to a
sustainable future for our business, our readers
and our planet. This book is made from Forest
Stewardship Council® certified paper.

ALFIE

Alfie's Christmas

Shirley Hughes

THE BODLEY HEAD

LONDON

Soon it would be Christmas time!

Alfie's little sister, Annie Rose, was too little to understand about Christmas, but Alfie was thinking about it a lot. He was making decorations, and cards to send to friends.

He had a calendar to help him count off the days. It had a picture of Baby Jesus and Mary and Joseph, and the shepherds and the angel, and the animals, and the three kings bringing presents, and the star shining above. They sang songs about it at Nursery School.

Alfie was helping with the cooking. He made some delicious biscuits in the shape of Christmas trees.

All the family went to the market to choose a real Christmas tree.
  "It's got to be just the right size," said Mum. "Not too big and not too small."
  They found one with beautiful spreading branches.

Alfie helped Dad to carry it into the living room. It smelled lovely. Then Dad fetched the big box of decorations from the attic.

They spent a lot of time arranging them on the tree. When they had finished, they switched on the fairy lights and left the curtains open so that all the people passing by could see it.

"To wish everyone a happy Christmas," said Mum.

Alfie and Dad set out on a special secret shopping expedition to buy Alfie's present for Mum. They spent a long time looking.

Dad thought that some nice-smelling stuff to put in the bath would be good. But in the end Alfie chose a beautiful necklace of blue beads.

Alfie helped Dad wrap up parcels. As well
as Mum's present there was one for
Great-Grandma Hilary and one for
Maureen MacNally, who lived across
the street and sometimes did babysitting,
and Grandma, and quite a lot of other
people too. Annie Rose liked
playing with the shiny
wrapping paper.

Now the house was full of secrets and packages that you were not allowed to look inside.

There was one thing which was carefully hidden, and that was Alfie's present for Dad. It was a very special flower pot which Alfie had decorated at Nursery School. In it was a tiny green shoot which was pushing up through the earth, and soon it would turn into a beautiful spring flower.

Mum helped Alfie to make a list of all the presents he wanted. It was quite a long list. Then she helped him write a letter to Father Christmas. Alfie drew a picture of himself to go with it and they put their address at the top.

Then they put it in an envelope with "To Father Christmas" written on it, and Mum helped Alfie post it in the pillar box at the end of their street.

"Will he get it all right?" Alfie wanted to know.

"Sure to," said Mum.

Christmas Eve came at last.

As it began to get dark, some carol singers came
to their street, and Mum and Alfie stepped outside to join in.

Alfie put a little plate of snacks on the hearthrug for Father Christmas in case he felt hungry. He was worried that their fireplace wasn't big enough for Father Christmas and his sack of presents to get through, but Mum said she was sure he'd manage somehow.

At bedtime Alfie hung up his stocking at the end of his bed. Annie Rose had hers on the chair near her cot.

Alfie's oldest, most favourite toy, Flumbo, had a little stocking of his own.

After Mum and Dad had tucked them up, Alfie lay awake for a long time because he was so excited. But at last he fell asleep.

When he woke up he knew it wasn't morning. It was the middle of the night. He could hear someone moving about in the room! Perhaps it was Father Christmas!

Alfie knew that he never left presents until all children were fast asleep, so he screwed up his eyes tight and hid under the duvet. Then he heard something dropping onto the floor. He sat up and peered into the darkness.

He could see that his stocking was bulging with surprises, but he knew it was not time to open them yet. Then he saw Annie Rose, wide awake. She had managed to get out of her cot and was sitting in the middle of the floor, opening all her presents, one by one!

Alfie called out and Mum came running. It took a long time before they all managed to settle down to sleep again.

The next time Alfie woke up, everything was quiet and he knew that Christmas morning had come at last.

Annie Rose was still asleep. Alfie opened his stocking presents, one by one. He was glad that he had waited till morning to unwrap them. There were some lovely things in there.

In Flumbo's stocking was a Father Christmas hat, a car, some sweets and a tiny notebook and pencil.

Now Christmas Day had really begun!

Alfie ran downstairs to look at the tree. And there, propped up against it, was a scooter! It was EXACTLY what he wanted. There was a smart helmet to go with it.

Annie Rose had a fairy dress
with wings. Mum and Dad were
very pleased with the presents
Alfie gave them. Mum put on her
blue beads straight away, and
Dad put his plant pot on the
windowsill where it would
get plenty of sunshine.

Soon after breakfast
the MacNally family from
across the street dropped
by to wish them all a
Happy Christmas.

Later Grandma arrived with Great-Uncle Will. He was her brother,
and he had come on a visit all the way from his home in Australia.
    "I'm hoping for snow, and lots of it!" he said.
    There was no snow, but the sun had come out.

Mum and Grandma set out for church. They took some cakes and sandwiches and some of Alfie's special biscuits to share with people who had no home to go to.

While they were out, Alfie and Annie Rose played with their new toys while Great-Uncle Will helped Dad to get the Christmas dinner ready.

Then they all sat down to eat together.

Afterwards Annie Rose was tired and cross and she needed a rest.

There was another small problem when Alfie and Dad discovered that the remote control of Alfie's new space buggy had no battery.

"I'll have to see if I can find one," said Dad.

Then Great-Uncle Will suggested that perhaps meanwhile he and Alfie might go out and test Alfie's new scooter.

When Alfie sped off along the pavement, Great-Uncle Will had to run very fast to keep up.

On the way home he told Alfie that in
Australia right now it was summertime,
and people were swimming in the sea
and having barbecues on the beach.
He said that there were parrots
flying about, and how once he had
seen a koala sitting at the top of
a gum tree near his back yard.

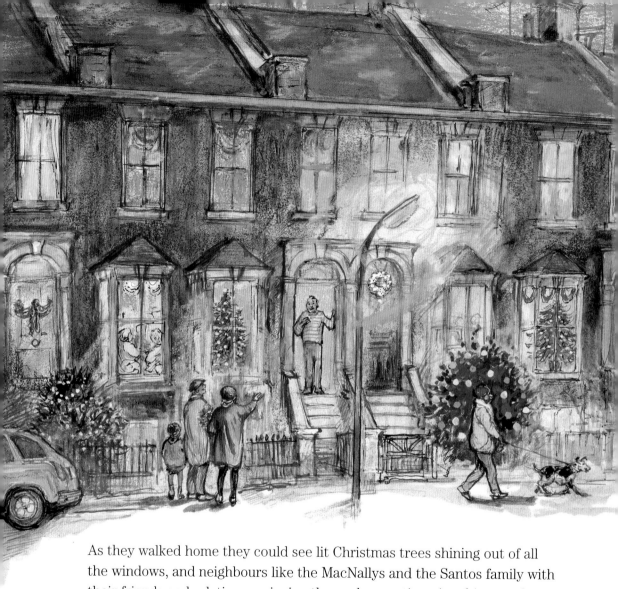

As they walked home they could see lit Christmas trees shining out of all the windows, and neighbours like the MacNallys and the Santos family with their friends and relations, enjoying themselves, eating nice things and watching television together.

When they got home they found Dad and Grandma on the front
doorstep with Annie Rose. She had woken up in a good mood and
was waving her fairy wand.

Dad had found a new battery.

"I like Christmas, don't you, Great-Uncle Will?" said Alfie.

"You bet," said Great-Uncle Will.